THE WORLD
OF CHAOS

KOMODO THE LIZARD KING

With special thanks to Michael Ford

To Art Gould

www.beastquest.co.uk

ORCHARD BOOKS
338 Euston Road, London NW1 3BH
Orchard Books Australia
Level 17/207 Kent St, Sydney, NSW 2000

A Paperback Original
First published in Great Britain in 2010

Beast Quest is a registered trademark of Working Partners Limited
Series created by Beast Quest Limited, London

A CIP catalogue record for this book is available from
the British Library.

ISBN 978 1 40830 723 6

10

Printed and bound by CPI Group (UK) Ltd, Croydon, CR0 4YY

The paper and board used in this paperback are natural recyclable
products made from wood grown in sustainable forests. The
manufacturing processes conform to the environmental regulations of
the country of origin.

Orchard Books is a division of Hachette Children's Books,
an Hachette UK company.

www.hachette.co.uk

KOMODO THE LIZARD KING

BY ADAM BLADE

THE ICY DESERT
KAYONIAN MARSHLANDS
KAYONIAN PLAINS
KAYONIAN FOREST

Kayonia
THE GOLDEN VALLEY
MEATON

Hail, young warriors!

Tom has set out on a Quest of his own choosing, and I have the honour of helping with magic learnt from the greatest teacher of them all: my master, Aduro. Tom's challenges will be great: a new kingdom, a lost mother and six more Beasts under Velmal's spell. Tom isn't just fighting to save a kingdom. He's fighting to save those lives closest to him and to prove that love can conquer evil. Can it? Tom will only find out by staying strong and keeping the flame of hope alive. As long as no foul wind blows it out...

Yours truly,

The apprentice, Marc

PROLOGUE

Badawi tugged up his scarf to cover his nose and mouth, and pushed headlong into a fresh storm that swirled across Kayonia's freezing desert. Grains of sand as cold as ice stung his eyes. Around him the rest of the tribe struggled onwards, huddled in their furs. The column of people and animals were tired after a long day's march.

Every year they made this journey to reach warmer lands where they could barter their furs and precious metals at market, and each year the journey was just as hard.

Some say there are places where deserts are scorched with heat! Badawi thought.

He knew they would reach the end of the desert in another day or so, then the horses could graze in comfort.

If we ever make it…

The tribe's stocky horses, laden with heavy goods for trading, lumbered along, harnesses clinking. Badawi's horse was moving more slowly than the rest. The fungus infecting his hooves was growing worse by the day.

Two mares had already been lost on this journey and their loads had been shared among the other horses. The foot disease eventually made it impossible for the animals to walk. There was no choice but to leave the animals where they fell. Badawi knew that if more horses perished, the tribe would be stranded in the desert.

Only one thing was known to cure the disease – the Black Cactus.

If we don't find it soon, thought Badawi grimly, *we're in real trouble.*

Without horses, they couldn't trade; and if they couldn't trade, the tribe would starve.

As ever in Kayonia, night fell suddenly. Darkness descended like a black shroud, as two of the three moons rose into the sky. The wind dropped. Badawi pulled the scarf from his mouth and watched his breath form frozen clouds.

From the head of the group came the sound of shouting, and a murmur passed back along the line.

"We've found it!" called a voice.

Badawi led his horse out of the line and up to where Edwin, the leader of the tribe, was pointing. Silhouetted against the glowing orb of the third moon was a shape that everyone in the tribe recognised.

The Black Cactus.

It stood as tall as a man. The outer branches reached to the sky like grasping fingers, and hundreds of sharp spikes glittered in the moonlight. Badawi dismounted and ran across the sand as quickly as he could. It would only take a few drops of the Cactus juice to cure the horses' infection. The tribe was saved!

But his companions stopped. They formed a semicircle, roughly twenty paces from the Cactus. Badawi paused beside them.

"What's the matter with you?" he asked.

The men looked from one to the other and finally Edwin spoke.

"You know what they say," said

the leader. "The Black Cactus is guarded by..."

"Nonsense!" said Badawi. "That's just a rumour to scare children."

Nobody moved.

"Fine," said Badawi. "If none of you has the courage to take a piece of the Cactus, it's up to me."

Still, as he walked towards the Cactus, his eyes searched the dark horizon, checking for attackers.

Nothing but sand. There's no monster here!

Badawi unsheathed his knife and knelt beside the Cactus. Its surface shone like ebony in the moonlight. Vicious spikes, each as long as his finger, but thin as a needle, jutted out. It was difficult to bring the knife close enough, but Badawi found a spot on one of the narrower branches. He used a sawing motion with his blade to cut into the flesh.

One of the tribe gasped. Before Badawi could turn, the sand beneath his knees seemed to lurch.

Badawi pitched forwards into the Cactus and the spikes tore open his sleeve, gouging his arm. He sucked air in through his teeth, trying not to cry out with pain.

The other tribesmen were backing away from him, looking on in fear. The ground shifted again under Badawi's feet, but this time he kept his balance. His eyes were fixed on the sand. Something pushed out from the swirling dune on the other side of the Cactus – a long, dark head with orange stripes running along a powerful jaw. Bulbous eyes swivelled onto Badawi as the rest of the body slithered out from the sand. Scaly black skin covered the Beast's hide and tail, crusted with orange warts. Its front claws and muscular hind legs thumped across the sand. A curved tongue darted from between its lips, tasting the air, hissing like red-hot metal plunged into water. Badawi's blood turned cold.

What they said was true. Komodo was real!

With a shake of its massive tail, the Beast charged at Badawi, who tripped backwards, dropping his knife. He heard shouts of terror from the rest of the tribe as they turned and ran.

Komodo stopped a few paces away from Badawi and reared up on his hindquarters, blotting out the moon. His throat inflated with a hiss and two flaps spread out like fans on either side of his face, flaring angry red.

Komodo's razor sharp front claws raked the air. Badawi cowered, too afraid to move. As the Beast lunged, the tribesman's screams ripped across the desert.

CHAPTER ONE

A NEW KINGDOM

Velmal stepped into the portal with Freya, preparing to depart the kingdom of Gwildor. Tom couldn't believe he had been reunited with his mother, only to have her snatched from him so soon. Freya cast a glance back at Tom before Velmal gave her an angry tug; the two of them were sucked down the swirling chute.

"No!" cried Tom, running towards

the coloured entrance to peer into the rainbow abyss. It was already beginning to shrink. He felt Elenna's hand on his shoulder, pulling him back.

"Are you sure about this?" she asked. "This portal could lead *anywhere*... You may never get home."

"I have to!" shouted Tom, as Storm and Silver gingerly inched over to them. "Freya's my mother..."

Elenna nodded. "Then we're coming, too."

Tom and Elenna turned to face the portal. "Ready?" he asked.

"Always," she replied.

Tom leapt into the magical tunnel, followed by his friends. The landscape melted away and Tom found his body flipping over in a powerful wind.

I'm falling... he thought. No, that wasn't right. There was no ground rushing up to meet him.

Tom twisted over in the air to right himself, and gazed at the rainbow colours spiralling on every side. The chute was as wide as four people laid head to toe. Something brushed his foot and he turned.

"Elenna!"

"Where is this taking us, Tom?" she shouted, struggling to form the words as the wind howled past her face.

"I don't know," Tom admitted. A frown of confusion creased Elenna's face, but she didn't look scared. Behind her Storm galloped in the air, the strange wind whipping his tail. Silver ran alongside, tongue lolling as he barked excitedly. But where was Velmal? And his mother?

As he turned to look ahead, a flicker of purple caught Tom's eye: Velmal's robes. The evil Wizard was drifting some distance away. He held Freya's arm in a vice-like grip. Her black hair was snaking around her head and Velmal's robes buffeted against the tide of air.

"I have to rescue my mother," Tom shouted to Elenna. He dived onwards into the tunnel of light. Invisible forces smashed into his body, threatening to throw him against the sides of the chute, but Tom pulled himself through the air as though fighting a tempest at sea, straining his shoulders and arms to hold steady.

He was gaining on Velmal, pulling ahead of Elenna and the animals. He gritted his teeth as he forced his body further down the tunnel. The evil wizard must have sensed him getting near and looked over his shoulder, snarling. Tom saw his hand tighten on Freya's wrist.

"Let her go!" Tom shouted.

Velmal laughed. "Never! She's made her choice and now she'll be my servant forever."

Tom's enemy drew himself upright, and hurled a crooked bolt of lightning towards him. Tom lifted his shield and felt the surge explode across the surface as a deafening thunderclap smashed his eardrums. Smoke fizzled all around him. Velmal's face darkened with fury.

"It'll take more than that to stop me!" Tom cried, and ploughed onwards, kicking with his legs.

Velmal turned away and hurled another ball of fire, but not at Tom.

Ahead, the side of the rainbow tunnel ripped open. The evil Wizard veered off towards the gap, dragging Tom's mother roughly alongside him.

With a final laugh, Velmal gripped the edge of the tear and climbed through. As she was also pulled out, Tom's mother threw him one last glance. Freya's mouth was twisted in a sly smile. Then she, too, was gone.

Doubt plunged through Tom's heart

as he continued down the chute. Perhaps Velmal was telling the truth, after all.

Is it too late for my mother? Tom wondered. *Is her heart completely clouded by dark magic?*

Tom reached the hole just as it sealed up. He slashed with his sword against the side, but it was no use. The blade passed through the multicoloured wall as if it were water. Tom growled in frustration as he slid helplessly by, pulled by the force of the magical tunnel.

Elenna appeared beside him, screwing up her eyes against the wind and pumping her legs to build up speed. She gripped his arm as a sudden blast threatened to smash her into the chute's wall.

"Are you all right?" he asked.

Suddenly the colours of the walls seemed to dim, and Tom saw blue sky beyond.

"What's happening?" he shouted.

The chute evaporated altogether and gravity seized him. This time he *was* falling.

Tom slammed into the ground and felt the breath driven from his lungs as he rolled over and over. Elenna cried out beside him.

Tom looked up to see Storm land far more gracefully, thundering across the grass, neighing triumphantly.

He climbed to his feet, checking himself for injuries. He picked up his sword and shield. Fields stretched all around, with grasses up to knee height. Mountains rose in the distance and a large, pale yellow sun hung directly overhead.

What strange new kingdom was this?

A thin whimper reached his ears.

"Silver!" said Elenna. She was already rushing towards the sound. Tom ran after her.

They found Silver behind a grassy hillock. He was lying on his side, cautiously sniffing at his foreleg and looking meekly at Elenna.

She knelt beside the wolf and stroked him above the ears.

"What's wrong, boy?" she asked. When she tried to touch his leg, he growled in pain and shifted a little. Tom could see that the lower leg bone was bent at an unnatural angle.

"Tom," said Elenna. "It's broken!"

CHAPTER TWO

A QUEST IN KAYONIA

Tom reached for the emerald in his belt. Its healing powers had helped them on their Quests many times. Tom held the emerald over Silver's injured leg, placing his other hand beneath the break to steady it. The wolf looked up and lifted his lip in a half-hearted snarl. Elenna stroked his head.

But nothing happened. The jewel remained cold and lifeless in his hand.

"Is something wrong?" Elenna asked.

Tom shook his head. "It's not working," he said. "There's some sort of...blockage."

"But it *has* to work," said Elenna. She snatched the jewel from Tom's hand and held it closer still to the broken limb. Nothing happened. Silver's fur trembled and he lay his head against the ground. Tears of frustration welled in Elenna's eyes. Tom prised the emerald slowly from her fingers.

"I'm the only one who can use the jewels," he said gently. "You know that."

Elenna pounded the ground with her fist. "Then why won't the jewel work?" she asked.

Tom brought the jewel over the leg again and closed his eyes.

I can't let Elenna down, he thought. *No one else can save Silver.* The jewel tingled in his hand.

"Yes!" gasped Elenna. "Tom, you're doing it!"

Tom opened his eyes and saw the bend in Silver's leg straightening. Green light from the emerald bathed

Elenna's face and his own. She turned to him with a delighted laugh.

Silver flexed his leg and then jumped up. He licked Tom's face gratefully and ran in a tight circle, barking with joy. Tom smiled back at Elenna, but his relief was tinged with anxiety. The magic had failed the first time. Why? He couldn't think of a reason.

Tom slipped the emerald back into place on his belt, and peered around, looking for any sign of Velmal and Freya. There were grassy rolling hills as far as Tom could see, with occasional outcrops of rocks, just like the Plains of Avantia.

"Where are we?" said Elenna.

Tom took the amulet from his neck and flipped it over. The map showing the landscape of Gwildor slowly blurred and then vanished altogether. He gasped as new lines appeared on the amulet's surface, showing the terrain and paths of this new kingdom. Writing swirled across the top of the image, as though scripted by an invisible hand. It spelled the word *KAYONIA*.

"I've never heard of Kayonia!" said Elenna.

"There's no reason you should have," said a deep voice. *Father?* Tom spun around. The images of Aduro and Taladon stood side by side. As a breeze blew across the grass, the outlines of the two figures shivered and faded a little. Behind them, Tom made out King Hugo's throne. A pang of loneliness shot through Tom's heart like an arrow; it seemed so long since he'd seen his homeland.

"Greetings, Tom and Elenna," said Aduro. "We had trouble finding you – you have travelled far from Gwildor."

Tom explained about the tunnel, and Velmal's escape.

"You have chosen this Quest, my son," said Taladon. "And it's up to you to complete it."

Tom's anger flared as he thought about Freya. "Were you ever going to tell me about my mother?" he demanded.

Taladon lowered his eyes. "There is much I have to tell you," he said. "About Freya, myself and many other things. And one day, I will… I promise…"

"Tom, there will be time for talking when you return to Avantia," Aduro said grimly. "For now, there is a Quest to contend with."

Tom felt his frustration fade away as he reminded himself that all of his questions could wait – right now, Freya needed him. "What am I to do on this new Quest?" Tom asked.

"Your mother's life lies in your hands, it's true," said Taladon. Tom heard his voice crack on the word 'mother'. *All these years without her must have been difficult for him,* Tom realised.

Aduro took up the story. "Here in Kayonia, six of Velmal's Beasts hold the key to Freya's recovery..." The wizard's voice trailed off as the vision flickered.

"Wait!" said Tom. "Tell me more."

The throne of King Hugo disappeared. Taladon and Aduro faded. Tom could just hear Aduro calling to them: "Fear not, Tom. I will send another."

Then they were both gone.

Tom felt Elenna's hand on his shoulder. "Don't worry," she said. "You've still got me."

Tom smiled back at her. He couldn't ask for better companions on his Quests. But who did Aduro mean by 'another'? From his tunic, Tom took out his magical compass. The needle swung from *Destiny* to *Danger,* then back again. It refused to settle on either, as though controlled by an invisible force. *Or Velmal,* Tom thought grimly. He was learning that he couldn't rely on the magic that had helped him through the other Quests.

He shook the compass again, but the needle drifted aimlessly.

"What does it mean?" Elenna asked.

Tom looked into her eyes. "It means we're on our own...for now."

CHAPTER THREE

TOWARDS THE ICY DESERT

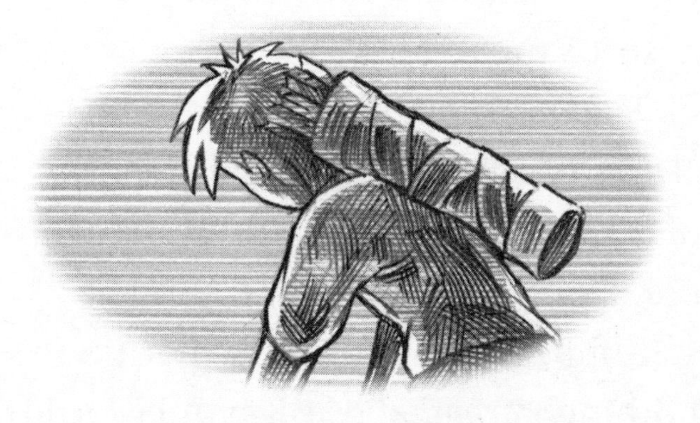

"Don't worry," said Elenna. "We don't need the compass. At least we have the amulet, and Aduro said we could always trust it, didn't he?"

Tom tucked the compass away briskly.

"He certainly did," he said, with more confidence than he felt. "And as long as we stick together, nothing

Velmal can send is our match."

He pulled out the amulet from the thong around his neck and held it on his palm. Their path snaked north, towards a land of shifting desert sands.

"That's strange," said Elenna. "Deserts are normally in the south of a kingdom – the northern parts are cool."

"I'm beginning to think that there's nothing *normal* about Kayonia," said Tom. As they looked at the amulet, the outline of a lizard appeared in the middle of the desert sands. The name 'Komodo' appeared beside it. Next to it was the outline of a cactus plant.

"I used to catch lizards with my uncle," said Elenna.

"I have a feeling this might not be so easy," Tom said. "Come on, let's go."

Tom placed a foot in Storm's stirrup and climbed into the saddle. He helped Elenna up behind him, and gripped the reins loosely. His stallion tossed his head.

"Looks like Storm's keen to go," laughed Tom.

He tightened his legs around Storm's flanks, urging him into a canter. Silver was already racing ahead, his pink tongue lolling from the side of his mouth. All sign of his injury was gone.

The terrain was hilly, but the way was smooth and Tom trusted Storm to avoid any obstacles that came into their path. It gave him time to think: who was this new helper that Aduro would send?

Tom and his companions made good time on their ride north. They reached a thin trickle of river, and Tom let Storm drink. Silver lapped eagerly at the water beside the stallion.

"If we keep up this pace," Tom said, "we'll reach the next Beast soon."

Suddenly, the Kayonian sun dulled from bright yellow to warm orange, like an egg yolk. It slid quickly across the sky, turning red.

"I've never seen a sun move so fast!" Elenna gasped.

Tom swallowed. His friend was right – the sun had been at its highest point when Taladon and Aduro had appeared. The temperature was dropping, too, and now Tom and Elenna were squinting into the dying rays of sunshine. By the time Tom slipped from the saddle, the glowing orb had been swallowed by the horizon. The sun had set in less time than it would have taken to fill his water flask.

As the sweat cooled on Tom's forehead, the sky became totally black. He could barely make out Elenna in the darkness. The sound of birdsong stopped dead, and Silver whimpered in fear.

"What now?" asked Elenna.

"We try to get some sleep, I suppose," Tom replied. "If night falls this quickly, who knows when the sun might rise again?"

Tom felt for Storm's saddlebag, stroking his horse's neck. He pulled out two blankets and handed one to Elenna, who looked like a shadow.

There was no way they could see to light a fire, or even find wood for one. Tom settled down onto the hard ground. He heard Elenna shifting restlessly beside him.

"Do you think we'll ever see Avantia again?" his friend asked. Her voice sounded small in the dark.

"I hope so," Tom replied. Above their heads, three moons became visible over the plains. "But one thing is certain," he added. "If we stay strong, we've at least a chance of defeating Velmal."

There was a flash of white as Silver yawned and showed his teeth.

Tom's stomach grumbled and he watched as the moons became silver like suspended coins. They glided in slow arcs across the sky. There were no stars.

Where has Velmal taken my mother? Tom wondered. The evil Wizard's twisted smile shone like a beacon in his mind's eye.

"While there's blood in my veins," he whispered, turning over to sleep, "I'll make him pay for what he's done."

CHAPTER FOUR

AN OLD FRIEND

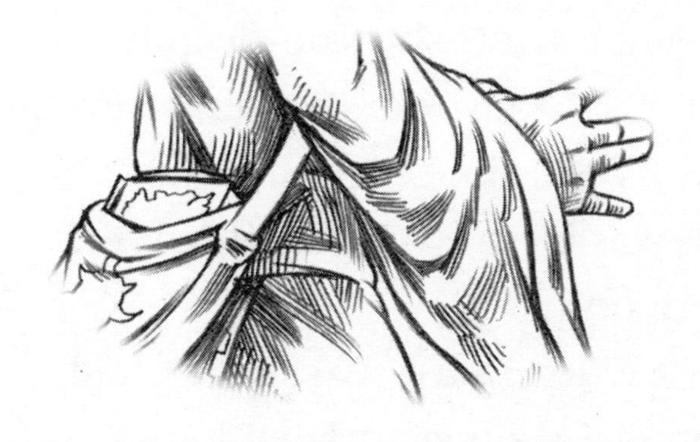

Daggers of light pierced Tom's eyelids, forcing him awake. Suddenly alert, he reached for his sword and scrambled to his feet. He squinted across their makeshift camp. The sun was climbing through the blue sky at astonishing speed, like a bubble rising through water.

Storm snorted and shook his mane in confusion. Elenna was lying on her front, her face buried into the crook of her elbow to shade her eyes. Tom sheathed his blade and shook his friend awake.

"What is it?" she said sleepily.

"Look!" said Tom, pointing into the sky. By the time Elenna sat up, the sun was already blazing down on them both.

"How long have we slept?" said Elenna, as Silver nuzzled her neck.

"I don't know," said Tom, stretching his arms. "But it didn't feel like a normal night, at all."

Silver suddenly shifted backwards on his paws and gave a low growl. Tom and Elenna spun around. Standing at the edge of the stream was a figure facing the other way. As he turned, Tom's hand tightened on his sword. Then he relaxed. *I know that face!* he thought.

"Marc!" Elenna gasped.

Aduro's apprentice grinned back.

"What are you doing here?" Tom asked in amazement.

Marc looked down at the water flowing over his feet.

"Oh dear!" he frowned. "It seems my magic is far from perfect."

Tom and Elenna both laughed as the trainee wizard stepped out of the babbling brook. They saw that his feet were as dry as tinder.

Clearly there are some benefits to being a wizard, Tom thought.

"And in answer to your question," Marc went on. "My master sent me."

"So that's what Aduro meant when he said he'd send another," said Elenna.

Marc's smile evaporated and his tone became serious. "I'm afraid I've been here for some time," he said. "I'm living at the castle of the warrior queen, the…" He paused. "The ruler of this kingdom."

"Something tells me it's not that simple," said Tom.

Marc nodded. "Now Velmal has arrived, Queen Romaine fears her throne is at risk. Why else would the evil Wizard come here? I'm helping her to plan her defences against any possible attack. It's not a matter of *if*, but *when*."

"And what about Freya?" Tom asked. He couldn't stop the words from escaping. He wanted to save Kayonia – but he was desperate to help her, too. "What about my… mother?"

Marc lowered his eyes.

"Tell me," said Tom. "Please."

"I'm afraid your mother's destiny is now in the hands of Velmal," said

Marc. "My magic has allowed me to see that she is terribly ill."

Tom clenched his fists – he had suspected something was wrong after seeing the awful sly look in her eyes. "Go on," he said.

Marc met his gaze. "Don't lose hope, Tom," he said. "There is a way to help Freya, a medicine for the poison that infects her."

Tom's heart beat a little faster. "What is it? I'll travel anywhere, do anything..."

"It's not one thing," said Marc gravely. "There are six. Six magical ingredients. When they are mixed together in a potion, we'll have our cure."

Tom sheathed his sword. "Then our mission is clear."

"Velmal won't let you complete this

task without great hardship," warned Marc. "As Aduro and Taladon warned you, Kayonia has Beasts, too – evil Beasts, who guard the ingredients."

"We've faced many Beasts before," said Tom. "This time will be no different."

"He's right," said Elenna.

Marc smiled. "Then good luck to you, heroes of Avantia." He faded slightly, as though lost in a cloud. "I must go, but before I forget…" Marc reached into a pocket in his robes and pulled out a small sack. "Some food to sustain you on your Quest." He tossed the sack to Tom, who reached out to catch it.

"Thank you," he said, but when he looked up, Marc had gone.

Tom opened the sack and found fresh bread, still warm from an oven far away. There was dried meat too, and three apples. Tom handed the bread to Elenna, who tore into it. Tom crunched into an apple, letting the juice fill his mouth. It had been two days since they'd last eaten.

Tom fed one of the two remaining apples to Storm.

"There you go, boy, you deserve a treat," he said. "Can't have grass all the time."

Elenna threw some meat to Silver, who pounced on it and chewed gratefully. They kept the rest of the food for later.

"Who knows when we'll be able to find more food?" said Tom.

After they'd drunk their fill of water from the stream and topped up their flasks, the joy of the meal faded. Tom's mind returned to the Quest.

So there would be Beasts to face, as always. But this time there was a greater task.

Tom placed his foot in Storm's stirrup and lifted himself into the saddle.

Elenna must have sensed his troubled thoughts.

"Are you OK, Tom?" she asked as she settled behind him.

Tom gripped the reins and turned Storm to face the path.

"I'm fine. I have to be," Tom said. "My mother is depending on me. I can't let her down."

CHAPTER FIVE

A DANGEROUS ENCOUNTER

Storm's flanks were soon soaked with sweat, but Tom didn't spare his stallion. This Quest was too important and he knew that Storm was strong enough to do him proud. The noise from Storm's hooves was deafening, and Tom was glad he didn't have to talk – his mind was focused on the pale face of his mother. Six more

Beasts would have to fall before he could help Freya. Six more battles in which he'd have to risk his life.

I'll fight Velmal's Beasts as often as I need to, he promised himself.

The air whistling past Tom's ears gradually became cooler, and he checked the map again to make sure they were still going the right way.

"Something isn't right," said Elenna. Tom felt her shiver behind him. "If we're heading towards a desert, shouldn't the air be warming up?"

As Silver raced beside them, he seemed fine – his thick fur usually kept out even the coldest winter weather – but Tom shivered.

"I don't understand, either," he said. "But we have to follow the map."

They set off again, and Tom felt the

biting wind cut into his tunic. Goose pimples pricked his skin, his knuckles were white where they gripped the reins, and his fingers were like numbed claws. Elenna hugged him tightly from behind to share their body heat. They reached the top of a hill and were rewarded with their first view of the Kayonian desert.

The sand below stretched all the way to the horizon: a bleak, empty expanse. Almost black in colour, the grains blew across the wilderness in clouds. Tom could hear the winds howling like a lonely wolf.

"Look!" said Elenna, pointing down the slope.

Tom saw a huddle of carts and covered wagons. There was smoke from a shielded fire. People crowded around the flames, warming themselves. A few others drifted around the small camp, checking the horses. All the people wore thick furs down to their ankles, with fur hats and scarves wrapped around their faces.

"Perhaps we can buy some extra clothing from them," Tom suggested.

"If they're friendly," Elenna replied nervously.

One or two of the people were casting glances at Tom and Elenna, but none made any move towards them.

"We don't have a choice," said Tom, nudging Storm in the direction of the camp. Silver padded beside them, panting from the long run.

Several of the tribespeople stood as Tom trotted down the slope with his companions. One man came forward and pulled his scarf away from his face. He was grey-bearded with tired eyes and a thin face.

He might be the leader, Tom thought. He pulled Storm to a halt.

"Greetings," he said to the stranger. He was so cold, it was hard to stop his teeth chattering.

The man stared at them, his eyes narrowing with suspicion. His gaze flicked to Tom's sword.

"Greetings to you also, travellers," replied the tribesman. "What brings you this way?"

"We seek something in the desert," Tom explained. "And some furs, if you have any spare."

The man seemed to relax.

"Furs we have," he said. "For the right price. But the desert holds nothing but death. Follow me."

Tom and Elenna dismounted and Tom led Storm through the camp by his reins. The other tribespeople shot them glances. Silver padded silently beside Elenna. The old man threw off one of the hemp-cloth coverings from a cart, and pulled out two patchwork fur jackets.

"These should fit you," he said. "And for payment?"

Tom looked to Elenna. Her lips had turned blue with cold. She reached into her tunic and pulled out three of the gold coins they had collected from the Rainbow Jungle. With trembling hands, she held them out to the tribesman. He took them, and tested each coin between his teeth, before nodding with satisfaction.

"Your gold is good," he said, and handed over the furs. Tom passed one to Elenna and put one on himself. The man's expression turned hard again – he obviously wasn't going to invite them to warm themselves by the fire.

Tom turned to go, but Elenna was looking at one of the horses standing nearby. She saw that they looked sick, and were stamping their hooves agitatedly.

"What's wrong with the horses?" she asked.

"Sick," said the tribesman. "Most of them are. Some sort of fungus in the hooves."

As they watched, one of the horses collapsed on its side, its eyes rolling in its head. Its breath came out in clouds as it lay on the icy ground. *If the horse lies there for much longer, it will freeze to death,* Tom realised.

"Poor thing!" said Elenna, rushing to the horse's side. "Can't you do something?"

"Nothing," said the older man. "Why do you think we're stuck here?"

Tears were springing up in Elenna's eyes as she stroked the animal's nose.

"Tom, you have to use your talon," she cried. "It's the only way…"

"A talon?" said the man.

Other members of the tribe crowded in behind him. "What's that, Edwin?" said a woman. "This boy can heal our horses, can he?"

Tom looked at Elenna, who was blushing. He couldn't blame her for revealing his secret – she was only concerned about the animals. Epos's talon healed cuts and bruises – could it also heal infections? Even if it could, Tom already knew that his special skills didn't always work in this new kingdom. If these people thought he was wasting their time...

I don't have any choice, Tom thought.

"I'll try to help," he said, taking the talon from his shield. One or two of the crowd were whispering in excitement. Tom knelt in the cold black sand and held the talon over the horse's damaged hoof. He closed his eyes and concentrated on channelling the magical power.

Nothing happened.

Tom tried again, but he could feel the magic wasn't working. He opened his eyes.

"I'm sorry," he said, scanning the anxious faces of the crowd.

The woman who had previously spoken huffed. "Made-up nonsense!"

As Tom slipped the talon back into

the shield, several of the tribespeople stared at his belt, which contained the sparkling jewels from his previous quests. Their eyes shone with greed.

"Come on, Elenna," said Tom. "It's time to go."

They got to their feet and backed away from the crowd, through the wagons and carts. No one tried to follow. Tom was beginning to think they'd escape without any trouble.

"I should have known the magic wouldn't work!" he murmured to Elenna. "Why did I even try?"

Suddenly he heard the hiss of a dagger being drawn behind him.

"Tom!" gasped Elenna.

Tom turned and saw a tribesman gripping his friend's arm and holding a dagger at her throat. He was a young man, thin with hunger, but Tom could see the muscles standing out on his chest and arms. Silver growled and bared his teeth, but knew better than to attack.

"You're not going anywhere," said the man. His blade sparkled in the sunlight, promising death. If Tom didn't act now, Elenna could die!

CHAPTER SIX

THE BLACK CACTUS

"What do you want?" Tom asked.

The man's eyes narrowed. "That belt will do for a start," he said, jerking his chin towards the jewels around Tom's waist. "Those stones will fetch a good price, maybe even enough to buy medicine to cure the horses."

The rest of the tribespeople were

gathering behind Tom. There was no way out. He could see these people were desperate.

"I can't give you the belt," he said. Without the power the six jewels bestowed, he might not be able to complete this Quest at all. He might lose his mother to Velmal for good.

"Then the girl dies," said the man. A trickle of blood ran down Elenna's neck, as the man pressed his blade harder.

"Don't give it to him!" said Elenna. "Don't give in, Tom."

I don't have a choice. Tom took a deep breath and began to unhook the belt buckle.

"Wait!" said Elenna. She was looking past him at someone in the crowd. Tom turned round.

The old man who'd met them

earlier stepped forwards. He squared his shoulders and gave a curt nod to the man holding Elenna.

"Are you the leader of this tribe?" Elenna asked.

"I am," said the man. "My name is Edwin."

"What if we help to heal your horses?" said Elenna. "Isn't that what you want?"

What's she up to? Tom wondered. *We already tried once, and it didn't work.*

"You've shown us how useless your 'magic' is," said Edwin. "Why should we believe you this time?"

"We could help you find the medicine you need," said Elenna. She cast a glance towards Tom that said: *Can't we?*

The woman who'd spoken before snorted. "There's nothing you can do, my girl," she said. "It's the Black Cactus that we need."

The Black Cactus! thought Tom, remembering the image on the amulet. *That's the ingredient we need, too.* He had to think quickly.

"I can get the Cactus for you," he said.

Several members of the tribe burst out laughing.

"You can't get *near* the Cactus," snarled the man holding Elenna. "We've already lost one of our number trying."

A murmur of agreement passed through the crowd. "Kill her!" someone shouted.

"All right," said Tom, hastily stepping forwards. "The belt is yours."

"No!" said Elenna. Tom ignored her. He had a new plan.

He unlooped the belt and threw it in a high arc towards Elenna's captor. As he hoped, the man loosened his grip and reached out to catch the belt. Elenna gritted her teeth and drove her elbow hard into the man's gut. With an *ooof,* he doubled over.

Tom sprang into action, using his shield to smash the dagger from the flailing man's arm, then he kicked his enemy's legs out from beneath him, sending him sprawling. Some in the crowd rushed forward, but Tom plucked up the dagger and held it at the man's chest.

"Stay back!" Tom shouted.

The crowd hesitated. Elenna appeared beside him with her bow pulled taut. Silver crouched close by her legs, growling.

"Good work," Tom said.

"Thanks," she whispered back.

Tom gave the man who had attacked Elenna a hard stare, but his anger was already cooling.

"Please," whimpered the attacker. "Don't kill me."

Tom turned to the crowd. Their faces were etched were fear. *These people aren't bad,* Tom thought. *They're just desperate to survive.*

He straightened and stabbed the blade of the man's dagger into the ground between himself and the others.

"We came here in peace," Tom said.

"And we'll leave the same way."

Edwin stepped forwards. "I'm sorry for our actions," he said gravely. "Please understand – we're desperate. Without our horses to take us to market, our tribe will die here in the desert."

Tom looked to Elenna. She lowered her bow.

"Can't we help them?" she said under her breath.

Her neck was still bleeding and for a moment Tom's anger flared. *These people tried to rob us!*

Then he heard Storm give a soft whinny nearby. He turned to see his stallion nuzzling the horse that had fallen onto its side.

"Very well," he said to the crowd. "I told you I'd get the Black Cactus, and I wasn't lying. We'll help you."

"Thank you," said Edwin. He took out the three gold coins Elenna had given him and held them out on his open palm. "Take these back. It's all we have to give."

Tom shook his head. These people needed the money more than he did.

"Come on," he said quietly to Elenna as he put on his belt. "We have a Quest to finish."

CHAPTER SEVEN

A DESERT TREK

Back in the saddle, Tom checked the amulet, and steered Storm towards the Black Cactus. Towards the Beast, too, judging by the map.

"This is the coldest desert I've ever visited," said Elenna from behind him. Tom turned and saw her lips were almost blue. The sun was a pale disc in the sky and it did little to warm the air.

"Even chillier than the Icy Plains of Avantia!" he replied, pulling his furs tighter where the cold wind seeped through.

The words of the tribesman echoed in Tom's head. *We've already lost one of our number.* He wondered: was that death an accident, or something more sinister? Just what sort of Beast was Komodo?

As they pushed on across the desert, they were forced to slow down. Storm's hooves slipped in the black sand, and Tom couldn't risk injuring his stallion. The tribespeople had said they were doomed without their horses. Tom would be as well.

The air became suddenly gloomy. Tom turned to the sun behind him and watched as it sank like a stone.

Not again!

The kingdom of Kayonia was pitched into darkness. The temperature dropped further. Silver howled in complaint and the sound drifted across the empty desert.

"What now?" Elenna said.

"We sleep," said Tom, slipping out of the saddle. He sat heavily in the sand – the grains felt like crystals of ice beneath his fingers.

"Thank goodness we have these furs," he said, as Elenna squatted beside him. Tom spread one out beneath them and lay down, placing his hands behind his head. Cold seeped into his bones. Two of the three moons were already out, glowing against the blackness. The third was forming slowly, like a ghost.

Silver nestled in between them. The warmth of his fur was comforting.

"We'll rescue Freya," said Elenna. "Don't worry."

At times like these, Tom was glad of a friend.

Dawn broke, sudden and bright. Tom was surprised he had managed to sleep at all.

As he loaded their furs into the saddlebags, his stomach growled.

No time for food now, he told himself.

He and Elenna mounted Storm. Sitting in the saddle, Tom pulled out the amulet and turned it over, gazing at the map on the back. He could see the path they'd been following drawing near to the tiny drawing of Komodo.

"We're close," he said. "Let's go and fight another Beast!"

They trotted on with Silver at their side, leaving deep prints in the black sand. It was still cold but the wind had dropped, so the chill had less bite. It wasn't long before they saw a row of silhouettes against the horizon.

"More nomads?" Elenna asked nervously.

Tom shook his head. "They're not moving," he said, nudging Storm on.

As they approached the shapes, Tom saw they weren't people at all. They were strange plants of different sizes, black as coal. One or two were as tall as a man, but most were much bigger, towering over the dunes. The branches were straight, and looked as though they were charred by fire. Silver spikes bristled, glinting as they caught the cold sunshine.

Icicles hung from them like crystals.

"The Black Cacti!" said Tom.

"They're beautiful!" said Elenna.

Tom jumped down from the saddle and ran to the first plant, trudging through the soft sand.

"Be careful!" said Elenna. "Perhaps we should check the amulet to see where the Beast is?"

Tom barely heard her. They'd found the ingredient he needed!

He unsheathed his sword and held the blade against a thin branch. This would be easy. Now he only needed to find five more ingredients and his mother would be well again...

Tom spotted something out of the corner of his eye and he spun around. Too late! A snake-like thing shot across his body and wrapped itself around the hilt of his sword.

"Tom!" Elenna cried.

No, not a snake. Tom fought to hold on to his sword as the glistening red tendril tried to tug it away.

A tongue!

Tom's feet slipped in the sand and he lost his grip on the hilt. Before he could stand, the tongue disappeared into the sand, dragging his precious sword with it.

"What was that?" he shouted to Elenna who was already stringing an arrow into her bow. Silver was pacing nervously in the sand beside her, unnerved.

Then the ground shifted beneath Tom's feet and he struggled to stay upright. The desert seemed to be moving. Something orange broke the surface – a long, coiled tail with black spots. Then the mammoth, muscular body of a giant lizard emerged, its skin broken by huge warts. Two front legs clawed at the sand as the Beast backed out of his hiding place. Each foot ended with dagger-like talons. A head heaved out of the dune, sending sand cascading over Tom.

The creature's eyes, lidless and staring, were furious. The Beast leapt into the air, locking his eyes on Tom. With a sound that was between a croak and a roar, their enemy's throat inflated like a ship's sail – flaring angry scarlet.

Elenna gasped, and Tom stumbled backwards.

It was Komodo!

Tom reached for his sword, but it wasn't there. It was buried in the freezing sand.

Komodo's tongue, red like scalded skin, flickered in and out, tasting the air. As the Beast's shadow fell over him, Tom knew that Komodo could sense his alarm. Fear ran through him. Could he survive the encounter with this Beast?

CHAPTER EIGHT

THE LIZARD KING

Tom rolled out of the way just in time as Komodo's mighty, scaled body crashed into the sand; a moment's hesitation and every bone in his body would have been crushed to dust.

Tom jumped to his feet and turned to make sure his companions were safe. Storm was stamping the sand with his front legs, Silver alert beside him. *Where's Elenna?* Tom asked himself.

The Beast lumbered around to face him. But without a sword, was he doomed?

A hiss sliced the air, but it didn't come from the giant lizard. Komodo suddenly thrashed and roared with pain, rearing up and revealing a pale yellow belly of soft scales. Tom spotted the shaft of an arrow sticking out from the top part of his tail.

"Tom!" shouted Elenna. "Catch!"

Komodo hissed menacingly, but Tom looked up and saw something spinning through the air towards him. He caught it by the handle and felt a flicker of relief.

Elenna's hunting knife.

He tossed the leather sheath aside. Now at least he had a weapon. The

Beast's skin rippled as he rose again. This time Tom was ready – he lunged forwards, trying to swipe across Komodo's exposed belly.

One of Komodo's clawed forelegs blocked Tom's strike and sent the knife spinning off into the sand. Pain flooded Tom's arm and he could barely lift it from his side.

All I have left is my shield, he thought.

Tom shrugged it off his shoulder and onto his left arm. Komodo's mouth opened wide to reveal teeth sharper than the Cactus spines. The Beast's eyes shone with hatred and behind those dark pupils, Tom saw only evil. This Beast was Velmal's creation, without doubt.

When Komodo lunged with its flat head, Tom took the impact on his shield. It was like being hit by a charging bull; the blow sent him reeling.

Tom couldn't see a way out; if he could get away, he might have a chance. He darted right, and when Komodo struck again, Tom spun to the left, trying to work his way around the back of the giant lizard. Komodo twisted, flicking his massive tail like a whip at Tom's head. He ducked and rolled underneath. When he righted himself, Komodo was already turning.

But the Beast didn't attack. His eyes rolled sideways in his head and Tom realised he was no longer the object of the Beast's attention.

Komodo's glance had landed on Storm and Silver.

With a kick from his powerful hindquarters, Komodo lumbered in the direction of Tom's animal companions, tongue darting in and out hungrily. His swaying, muscular tail scored grooves in the black sand.

"No!" Tom shouted, giving chase.

Silver advanced bravely, placing himself firmly between Komodo and Tom's stallion. But it was hopeless.

Like a mouse facing a cat, Tom thought desperately.

A few paces to the side of the animals, Elenna loosed arrow after arrow towards the advancing Beast. But the wart-covered scales were thick as chain mail, and the shafts simply bounced off. Each arrow only fuelled Komodo's rage.

"Hey!" yelled Tom. "Stop! It's me you want." Komodo ploughed on through the black sand. "Curse you, Velmal!" Tom added in desperation.

The words seemed to do the trick. Komodo stopped dead, then turned slowly.

"I knew you were Velmal's creature!" Tom cried.

Elenna ran over to be with Silver and Storm. Grabbing the stallion's reins, she led them away.

Komodo came at him once more, and Tom ran in the opposite direction, luring him on. Charging through the thick sand was almost impossible – each step seemed to suck his feet down, and Tom's chest burned. Sweat burst from his pores and he shrugged off his fur. His skin cooled in an instant, but at least he could now move more easily.

Komodo had no such problems: his massive tail powered him over the desert surface in a straight line.

I've no chance on two feet, Tom realised. *But what about on four?*

Storm was fifty paces away, so Tom changed his course to a wide circle. He knew Komodo was close on his heels.

Twenty paces.

"I'm coming!" Tom shouted to Storm. "Hold on, boy."

His stallion must have understood, because he shifted slightly in the sand, so that he was facing away from Tom.

Ten paces.

The Beast was only a fraction behind, its breath rasping.

Tom reached for Storm's rump and leapt. Placing both palms on the horse's backside, he vaulted into the saddle. He kicked Storm's flanks and the stallion lunged forwards, churning sand. Komodo's teeth snapped shut, a hand's breadth from Storm's hind legs.

Now the chase was really on.

Storm galloped across the desert, with Komodo in hot pursuit. Tom glanced back. Showers of icy sand billowed up from Komodo's swaying tail. Anger blazed in his bulbous eyes and his orange skin flared. The distance between them was shrinking.

You're fast in a straight line, Tom thought. *But how about when you turn?*

Tom yanked Storm's reins left. The Beast roared and from the corner of his eye Tom saw him struggle clumsily to turn. Komodo lost ground. Tom steered a sudden right. Again, the Beast floundered.

"So you *have* got a weakness!" he yelled over his shoulder.

He led Komodo in a series of zigzags across the desert. The Beast began to tire. It was taking him longer and longer to right himself with each turn. Tom tugged the reins around a final time, making Storm perform almost a full circle. It was too much for Komodo. With an angry hiss the massive lizard's body tipped onto one side, then crashed upside down into the sand.

Tom saw his chance, and galloped alongside the stricken Beast. Komodo was squirming to right himself, as Tom leapt from Storm's saddle and seized the tail. It was as wide as his waist.

"Got you!" he cried.

Komodo snapped his jaws in frustration, swinging his tail from side to side. Tom held on, gritting his teeth. While he had the tail, he was safe from the Beast's deadly mouth and claws.

The thrashing stopped. Tom tightened his grip on the tail as Komodo went rigid. Seconds passed… Then Komodo lumbered away. But something was wrong.

I'm still holding the tail! Tom thought.

The Beast's tail had come off! Tom remembered the lizards in Errinel, his home village. They detached their tails from their bodies when distressed: Komodo was no different.

Tom cursed. As he watched Komodo run out of reach across the icy wastes of the desert, there was only one question that turned over and over in his mind. *What now?*

CHAPTER NINE

INTO THE ABYSS

Elenna ran to Tom's side with Silver racing after her. Rooting in Storm's saddlebag, she pulled out a rope and tied it to the end of an arrow.

"What are you doing?" he asked. "Komodo's getting away."

"Not for long," she said.

As soon as the arrow was placed in her bow, Tom understood. "Good thinking!" he said.

Elenna quickly focused the shaft on the Beast and released the arrow. It sailed in a shallow arc, trailing the rope in its wake, and thwacked into the lizard's leathery hide. Finally, an arrow had hit home! The other end of the rope lay in the sand, uncoiling like a snake as the Beast charged away, bellowing in anger.

It was almost out of sight.

Tom reached down, ignoring the pain in his arm, and grabbed the end of the rope. He wrapped it twice around his wrist and braced himself.

"Good luck!" said Elenna.

Before Tom could reply, the rope snapped taut and he was yanked off his feet, face first into the cold sand. It filled his mouth and eyes. For a moment Tom panicked. He spluttered and tried to blink the grains away.

The course sand grazed his arms as he was dragged headlong, its iciness numbing his flesh.

Tom managed to squirm onto his back. The pace didn't slacken. The rope burned around his wrist, but he didn't let go.

There's no way you're getting away from me, Komodo!

Tom twisted again so he was ploughing through the sand on his knees. With great effort he put his shield under his knees, gingerly stood up on it and, kicking up sand, he skied across the desert.

Hand over hand, Tom pulled himself closer to the running Beast, shortening the length of rope between them. He was being dragged up an incline to the top of a dune, and he couldn't see beyond it. Komodo

thrashed his hindquarters from side to side, trying to free the arrow's tip and throw off his unwelcome passenger, but it held firm. Tom's shoulders were screaming in pain with the effort of holding the rope.

This is getting me nowhere, he thought. *Even if I catch the Beast, I haven't got a sword to fight him.*

Suddenly the Beast veered left. Tom's momentum kept him moving

forwards towards the top of the dune as the rope between him and his enemy slackened. Then Tom realised why Komodo had turned. The desert ended, and the land dropped away.

It wasn't a dune. It was a cliff!

He was sliding straight for the edge.

The rope tightened again, and Tom felt his body snap around. One foot skidded off the edge of the cliff, spraying pebbles, and for a split-second he caught sight of the dizzying vista below. The rock face plummeted into an abyss deeper than any canyon in Avantia.

Tom balanced precariously on one foot as the other swung over the drop, then found himself tugged along behind the massive Beast; if he had gone any further over he would have fallen to his doom.

But the terrifying sight had given him a plan. He let go of the rope and ground to a halt in the rut gouged out by Komodo's passage.

The Beast barely seemed to notice and continued carving his path through the black sand. Tom pulled his shield out in front of him.

If I can make him come to me, then I have a chance.

With his free hand, Tom thumped

the surface of the shield as loudly as he could.

The Beast slowed.

"Come back here!" Tom yelled. He struck the shield again and the sound echoed across the desert.

Elenna, mounted on Storm, was trotting towards him.

"Tom," she shouted. "What do you want me to do?"

She was still too far away to see the edge of the cliff, Tom realised.

"Stay back," he called. "I know what I'm doing!"

He smacked the shield with an open hand. Komodo's walk became a run. Behind Tom, the wind whistled up from the depths of the gorge. He felt as though he was standing on the very edge of the world.

"Come on, you brute!" hissed Tom

through his teeth.

The Beast charged on – his muscular body must have weighed as much as a fully loaded cart, pulled with the power of four horses – all of it aimed straight at Tom. The skin of Komodo's throat inflated and his jaws opened wide to swallow up his prey.

Tom held firm until he saw his own reflection in the Beast's shiny eyes, then he threw himself to one side. Not far enough! He caught a whiff of Komodo's rotten breath as the Beast's flank slammed into him, tearing his skin with rough scales. Tom cried out in pain and tumbled over, clawing with his hand for any sort of hold. Elenna's scream cut through the sound of Komodo's roars and the world spun around. Tom's fingers closed on something hard, and his elbow jarred.

He opened his eyes – he was hanging from a jutting rock. Beneath him was empty space. Empty but for Komodo falling. The Beast angrily snapped its jaws. Tom wanted to look away, but couldn't. When Komodo hit the ground, a great cloud of dust enveloped him for a moment, fading away to reveal the Beast looking up at Tom.

Will this Beast never *die?* Tom wondered, as he stared down at his foe.

But then a low groan drifted up to his ears. Below, Komodo staggered and lurched. He toppled over like a broken tree, hitting the ground with a dull thud.

Komodo was dead. The first Quest was over.

Not quite, Tom thought. *I've still got to make sure* I *don't fall.* He managed to swing another hand onto the rock face, and heaved himself up a fraction. An arm appeared over the edge and gripped his wrist. It was followed by a smiling face. Elenna.

"You're alive!" she said.

"Just about," Tom half-grinned, half-grimaced. His clothes were torn down one side, and a long red cut bloodied his ribs where the Beast's scales had scraped past him.

Elenna pulled him up to safety.

"When I saw you go over, I thought that was it...I thought you were..."

"Me too," he said, sinking into the sand, exhausted.

"Look!" said Elenna, peering over the edge of the cliff. "Komodo!"

Tom's heart sank. *There's no way that Beast has got up* again!

He saw Elenna peering over the edge and he scrambled to join her.

At the bottom of the cliff face the dust had cleared. There was no sign of Komodo, but hundreds of smaller lizards were scurrying over the ground where the Beast had fallen.

The giant lizard that had stalked the Kayonian desert was gone for good.

CHAPTER TEN

AN UNWELCOME VISITOR

Silver was digging frantically in the sand near the Black Cactus plants. Tom leant a hand and soon found his sword.

"I told you he had the best nose in Avantia," said Elenna, scratching her wolf behind the ears.

"The best in Kayonia and all the kingdoms!" Tom replied. He shook off the sand, glad to feel the familiar hilt, now cold as ice, in his palm. "There's just one more thing to do." Tom strode over to one of the Cacti.

With a swing of the blade, he chopped off a branch from the plant, then, holding it carefully, stripped the deadly spikes with the sharp edge. That would be plenty of medicine for the nomads.

Enough for my mother too, when Marc comes, Tom thought.

The sand began to shift – two footprints formed.

"Marc's right on time," said Elenna, stepping forward to meet their friend.

But as a shape appeared, Tom realised it was taller than Aduro's apprentice. He recognised the purple cloak. Elenna suddenly stopped in her tracks.

"Velmal!" she gasped.

Storm stamped his front hoof in the sand, shaking his mane.

Tom's heart raced as another figure appeared beside the evil Wizard. Lying on the ground at his feet, propped up weakly on one elbow, was Freya. Her armour, battered and scarred, had dimmed to grey, and her jet-black hair hung limply over her face.

"Mother?" Tom said, falling to his knees.

Tom caught a glimpse of Freya's pale face. Her eyes were lacklustre and he couldn't tell whether or not she was focusing on him.

"You see, Tom," said Velmal. "You may have defeated Komodo, but your pathetic Quest will soon come to an end."

Tom tried to calm his grief and anger. "I won't give up," he replied. "Not while my mother lives."

"Your mother's life is in my hands," Velmal jeered, "and I will extinguish it like a candle when I please."

"We won't let you!" shouted Elenna.

Tom's hope seeped away, leaving him hollow.

Is Velmal right? Is there nothing we can do to stop him?

"Don't listen to him," said a friendly voice.

Tom turned slowly and saw Marc standing in the sand behind him. The young wizard was holding a small black cauldron in his hands.

"As long as you continue on the Quest, Velmal cannot win," he added. He held out the cauldron. "Place some of the Cactus juice inside."

Tom walked towards Marc, only for Velmal to step into his path, his fists clenched. Tom didn't stop and his skin tingled as he passed through the vision of the evil Wizard. Meeting Velmal's hate-filled gaze, Tom twisted the piece of Cactus over the cauldron. A few drops of the precious juice dripped inside.

"That's enough," said Marc. "I must go now. The Warrior Queen needs me."

"Yes, run away, apprentice," hissed

Velmal. "And tell her that I will have her kingdom, or see it destroyed."

But Marc was gone.

Tom took out his sword and pointed the blade at the cruel sorcerer.

"While there's blood in my veins," he shouted, "you'll never triumph in Kayonia!"

Velmal's face twisted with scorn, and he placed a bony hand on Freya's shoulder.

"Brave words, boy," he said. "But you'll never leave this kingdom alive. You and your mother will both perish here!"

Elenna came to Tom's side, along with Silver and Storm. Together they faced their enemy.

"I'm prepared for anything," said Tom. He took hold of Storm's reins and jumped into the saddle.

"Ready?" he said to Elenna.

"Let's get this medicine to the nomads," she replied, climbing behind him. "We can return our furs to them, too."

Velmal waved a hand. A gust of black sand blew and when it had passed, both he and Freya were gone.

Turning Storm to face the desert, Tom knew that the Quest in Kayonia had only just begun.

Here's a sneak preview of Tom's next exciting adventure!

Meet

MURO THE RAT MONSTER

Only Tom can free the Beasts from Velmal's wicked enchantment...

PROLOGUE

The hot sun shone down on the golden cornfields of the Kayonian Plain, the crops bending and swaying at the command of a light breeze.

Roland gazed into the sky. The days and nights were unpredictable in Kayonia, and the sun could set at any moment.

I'd better get moving, he thought.

Across the vast cornfields, other farmers were gathering their share of the crop. Roland didn't want to lag behind.

He had seen many harvests, but this seemed to be the best in years. The ears of corn carried plump grains. When these kernels were ground at the village windmill, they would make flour that the villagers could sell.

Roland raised his crescent-shaped scythe. He sang an ancient harvest song to himself as the blade sliced through the cornstalks. *"Hey-yah! The day is soon done! Hey-yah! Let us work while we can, for the sun is soon gone!"* The corn fell at his feet as he walked through the field, swinging the scythe.

"Urgh!" Roland suddenly choked. A foul, rotting stench caught at the back of his throat. He looked around. There was nothing except a sea of golden corn.

A rustling disturbed the cornstalks. It sounded like the mice that plagued the grain stores in the village – but much, *much* louder.

Something jumped out of the corn and landed on Roland's foot. It was a fat grey rat, staring at him with beady red eyes.

Roland shooed the rat away. He shuddered as more of the mangy creatures appeared. His skin crawled at the sight of their naked tails and long brown claws.

Follow this Quest to the end in MURO THE RAT MONSTER.

Win an exclusive Beast Quest T-shirt and goody bag!

Tom has battled many fearsome Beasts and we want to know which one is your favourite! Send us a drawing or painting of your favourite Beast and tell us in 30 words why you think it's the best.

Each month we will select **three** winners to receive a Beast Quest T-shirt and goody bag!

Send your entry on a postcard to
BEAST QUEST COMPETITION
Orchard Books, 338 Euston Road, London NW1 3BH.

Australian readers should email:
childrens.books@hachette.com.au

New Zealand readers should write to:
Beast Quest Competition, PO Box 3255, Shortland St, Auckland 1140, NZ or email: childrensbooks@hachette.co.nz

Don't forget to include your name and address.
Only one entry per child.

Good luck!

Fight the Beasts, Fear the Magic

www.beastquest.co.uk

Have you checked out the Beast Quest website? It's the place to go for games, downloads, activities, sneak previews and lots of fun!

You can read all about your favourite beasts, download free screensavers and desktop wallpapers for your computer, and even challenge your friends to a Beast Tournament.

Sign up to the newsletter at www.beastquest.co.uk to receive exclusive extra content and the opportunity to enter special members-only competitions. We'll send you up-to-date info on all the Beast Quest books, including the next exciting series which features four brand-new Beasts!

- [ ] 1. Ferno the Fire Dragon
- [ ] 2. Sepron the Sea Serpent
- [ ] 3. Arcta the Mountain Giant
- [ ] 4. Tagus the Horse-Man
- [ ] 5. Nanook the Snow Monster
- [ ] 6. Epos the Flame Bird

Beast Quest:
The Golden Armour

- [ ] 7. Zepha the Monster Squid
- [ ] 8. Claw the Giant Monkey
- [ ] 9. Soltra the Stone Charmer
- [ ] 10. Vipero the Snake Man
- [ ] 11. Arachnid the King of Spiders
- [ ] 12. Trillion the Three-Headed Lion

Beast Quest:
The Dark Realm

- [ ] 13. Torgor the Minotaur
- [ ] 14. Skor the Winged Stallion
- [ ] 15. Narga the Sea Monster
- [ ] 16. Kaymon the Gorgon Hound
- [ ] 17. Tusk the Mighty Mammoth
- [ ] 18. Sting the Scorpion Man

Beast Quest:
The Amulet of Avantia

- [ ] 19. Nixa the Death Bringer
- [ ] 20. Equinus the Spirit Horse
- [ ] 21. Rashouk the Cave Troll
- [ ] 22. Luna the Moon Wolf
- [ ] 23. Blaze the Ice Dragon
- [ ] 24. Stealth the Ghost Panther

Beast Quest:
The Shade of Death

- [ ] 25. Krabb Master of the Sea
- [ ] 26. Hawkite Arrow of the Air
- [ ] 27. Rokk the Walking Mountain
- [ ] 28. Koldo the Arctic Warrior
- [ ] 29. Trema the Earth Lord
- [ ] 30. Amictus the Bug Queen

Beast Quest:
The World of Chaos

- [ ] 31. Komodo the Lizard King
- [ ] 32. Muro the Rat Monster
- [ ] 33. Fang the Bat Fiend
- [ ] 34. Murk the Swamp Man
- [ ] 35. Terra Curse of the Forest
- [ ] 36. Vespick the Wasp Queen

Beast Quest:
The Lost World

- [ ] 37. Convol the Cold-Blooded Brute
- [ ] 38. Hellion the Fiery Foe
- [ ] 39. Krestor the Crushing Terror
- [ ] 40. Madara the Midnight Warrior
- [ ] 41. Ellik the Lightning Horror
- [ ] 42. Carnivora the Winged Scavenger

Beast Quest:
The Pirate King

- [ ] 43. Balisk the Water Snake
- [ ] 44. Koron Jaws of Death
- [ ] 45. Hecton the Body Snatcher
- [ ] 46. Torno the Hurricane Dragon
- [ ] 47. Kronus the Clawed Menace
- [ ] 48. Bloodboar the Buried Doom

Beast Quest:
The Warlock's Staff

- [ ] 49. Ursus the Clawed Roar
- [ ] 50. Minos the Demon Bull
- [ ] 51. Koraka the Winged Assassin
- [ ] 52. Silver the Wild Terror
- [ ] 53. Spikefin the Water King
- [ ] 54. Torpix the Twisting Serpent

Beast Quest:
Master of the Beasts

- [ ] 55. Noctila the Death Owl
- [ ] 56. Shamani the Raging Flame
- [ ] 57. Lustor the Acid Dart
- [ ] 58. Voltrex the Two-Headed Octopus
- [ ] 59. Tecton the Armoured Giant
- [ ] 60. Doomskull the King of Fear

Beast Quest:
The New Age

- [ ] 61. Elko Lord of the Sea
- [ ] 62. Tarrok the Blood Spike
- [ ] 63. Brutus the Hound of Horror
- [ ] 64. Flaymar the Scorched Blaze
- [ ] 65. Serpio the Slithering Shadow
- [ ] 66. Tauron the Pounding Fury

Beast Quest:
The Darkest Hour

- [ ] 67. Solak Scourge of the Sea
- [ ] 68. Kajin the Beast Catcher
- [ ] 69. Issrilla the Creeping Menace
- [ ] 70. Vigrash the Clawed Eagle
- [ ] 71. Mirka the Ice Horse
- [ ] 72. Kama the Faceless Beast

Special Bumper Editions

- [ ] Vedra & Krimon: Twin Beasts of Avantia
- [ ] Spiros the Ghost Phoenix
- [ ] Arax the Soul Stealer
- [ ] Kragos & Kildor: The Two-Headed Demon
- [ ] Creta the Winged Terror
- [ ] Mortaxe the Skeleton Warrior
- [ ] Ravira, Ruler of the Underworld
- [ ] Raksha the Mirror Demon
- [ ] Grashkor the Beast Guard
- [ ] Ferrok the Iron Soldier

All books priced at £4.99.
Special bumper editions priced at £5.99.

Orchard Books are available from all good bookshops, or can be ordered from our website: www.orchardbooks.co.uk, or telephone 01235 827702, or fax 01235 8227703.

Series 6

BEAST QUEST

Can Tom and his companions rescue his mother from the clutches of evil Velmal...?

978 1 40830 723 6

978 1 40830 724 3

978 1 40830 725 0

978 1 40830 726 7

978 1 40830 727 4

978 1 40830 728 1

978 1 40830 735 9

Does Tom have the strength to triumph over cunning Creta?

Series 7: THE LOST WORLD

OUT NOW!

978 1 40830 729 8

978 1 40830 730 4

978 1 40830 731 1

978 1 40830 732 8

978 1 40830 733 5

978 1 40830 734 2

FROM THE DARK, A HERO ARISES...

Dare to enter the kingdom of Avantia.

A new evil arises in Avantia. Lord Derthsin has ordered his armies into the four corners of Avantia. If the four Beasts of Avantia can find their Chosen Riders they might have the strength to challenge Derthsin. But if they fail, the land of Avantia will be lost forever...

FIRST HERO, CHASING EVIL, CALL TO WAR, FIRE AND FURY. OUT NOW!